Hannah's Helpers

Emilie Boon

PICTURE CORGI

PICTURE CORGI BOOKS

One day when everyone was asleep,
Hannah woke up early.
'What a mess!' she thought. 'I know, I'll tidy up.'

'It isn't much fun to clean up alone,' thought Hannah.
So she called all her friends and asked them to come
and help.

Hannah didn't have to wait long. With a bang and a beep, and a roar and a squeak, a car full of friends arrived.

Hannah opened the door and her friends marched in.
'Hello,' they said. 'Where's the mess?'

'Hush!' said Hannah. 'We mustn't wake the baby.'
She told them where to start and they tiptoed off to work.

They washed the windows,

they scrubbed the baby's dirty clothes,

they did the dusting, and tidied up the toys.
But they soon forgot about keeping quiet.

In the kitchen, dishes clattered.
The duck splashed in the sink and the cat broke a cup.
'Watch out!' said Hannah.

Upstairs in the bathroom her friends were singing as they worked.

'This is fun!' said the pig.

'Whoopee!' quacked the duck.

'Shhh,' said Hannah.

But it was too late. There was a cry from the bedroom.
The baby was awake!

'Quick!' said Hannah. 'Back to the car!'

The animals piled into the car and said, 'Goodbye!'
'Goodbye,' said Hannah. 'Thanks for all your help.'

'Come again soon!' she called, as her friends roared away.
Then she went back inside.

'Oh Hannah!' said her mother. 'What a lovely surprise!
Everything looks so clean and tidy!'

'What a clever girl! Did you do this all by yourself?'
'I did have a little help from my friends,' said Hannah.